THE
NOT IN HERE
STORY

Tracey Zeeck

pictures by David Bizzaro

penny
candy
BOOKS

Penny Candy Books
Oklahoma City & Savannah
© 2016 Penny Candy Books

 This book is printed on paper certified to the environmental and social
standards of the Forest Stewardship Council™ (FSC®).

Design: Shanna Compton, shannacompton.com

Photo of Tracey Zeeck by Shevaun Williams
Photo of David Bizzaro by Brandon Bales

20 19 18 17 16   1 2 3 4 5
ISBN-13: 978-0-9972219-2-3

Books for the kid in *all* of us
www.pennycandybooks.com

Dedication

To Charlie, Andy, Catherine, Debbie, Jeff, Uncle Gene, Father Marlin, Dr. Stanford, St. Anthony Hospital, William, Jennifer, Sabra, Blake, Jennette, Wayne, Linda, Mike, Jay, Jonathan, uncles, aunts, cousins, "godsiblings," and the good friends who carried us in their hands and hearts throughout the ups and downs. To Catholic Charities, and to all whose lives have been built upon the undeniably amazing foundation of adoption.

On a tree-lined street in a charming little city
lived two people who had nobody around to call them
"Mommy" or "Daddy,"

so they went by their other-people names,
Mr. and Mrs. Seek.

Although the Seeks had a very happy and full life, with everything they needed, one day they woke up and felt an interesting new feeling. A *weird* feeling. An *emptyish* feeling.

Something was missing. Something important.

Someone important.

They had everything they needed, sure, but they wanted someone else to share their life with.

"It's a baby that's missing from our home!"
Mr. and Mrs. Seek declared.

People had babies all the time. It seemed like everyone had one, everywhere they went.

Why just the other day, the Goodwins down the street brought home two! Mrs. Goodwin had a very large tummy before, but when she came home, not so big. And, *two* babies!

This was going to be easy as pie, they thought.

They went about their daily lives, confident they could grow a baby in Mrs. Seek's tummy.

After a while, Mr. Seek said, "Maybe you should check your tummy now."

"Great idea!" she exclaimed.

She looked down, shook her head, "Nope. Not in here."

Days passed. Weeks passed. Months passed.

But no baby appeared in Mrs. Seek's tummy. How could they find a baby if it wasn't in Mrs. Seek?

Maybe this wasn't as easy as they first thought.

Chip

Norbit

Grandma

Mr. M   Mrs. a   Mr. B

Mr. R

Uncle Fred

Guy

M. Bones

Mommy & Daddy

Mrs. Muscle

Miss. Filbert

Plus, now that they had announced their search, everyone was calling, wanting to know when that baby would appear.

Family, friends, even strangers had to know. This made the search even harder. They all told the Seeks where to look.

But no matter what they did, no matter how hard they went about their daily lives, the baby never appeared in Mrs. Seek's tummy.

The Seeks were sad. Their friends and family were sad, too. This made the Seeks even sadder.

Mr. Noodler

aunt Frank

Cousin frank

The Crispers

Harold

the Chesters

So they decided to take a vacation. Somewhere far away from their charming little city, which suddenly seemed like a cruel big city.

Somewhere far away from the help of all
the well-intentioned baby experts.

They both loved the desert—maybe if they went there to relax, the baby would get into Mrs. Seek's tummy. So off they went.

It took a while, and when they finally got there, it was very hot. That didn't slow them down. They visited the saguaros, the sand dunes, the trails, and had a lovely time. They even bought a little cactus souvenir to take home.

"Did you check your tummy?" asked Mr. Seek. Mrs. Seek looked down and shook her head, "Nope. Not in here."

So they moved on.

They both loved the mountains, so why not there? Maybe if they did some hiking, a baby would find its way into Mrs. Seek's tummy.

Up, up they went. When they got there, it was very cold. But that didn't stop them. They visited the ski slopes, the village, the chilly stream, and had a lovely time. They even bought a little pine tree as a souvenir.

"Did you check your tummy?" asked Mr. Seek, once more, with just the tiniest bit of hesitation.

Mrs. Seek looked down, and she shook her head a little longer this time before saying, "Nope. Not in here."

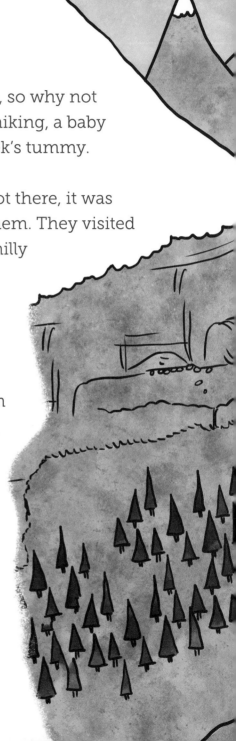

But the Seeks weren't ones to give up easily, and they decided to keep going. They both loved the jungle, so perhaps some exploring would encourage their baby to grow in Mrs. Seek's tummy.

Off they went. When they got there, it was very soggy. But that didn't stop them. They visited the canopy, the waterfalls, the rumbly volcano, and had a lovely time. They even bought an orchid as a souvenir.

"Did you . . . uh . . . check your—" began Mr. Seek.

"Nope," interrupted Mrs. Seek, looking down and shaking her head, "Nope. *Still* not in here."

She didn't even try to smile. She didn't feel happy. She felt like no matter where they went or what they did, no baby would ever get in her tummy.

That they'd never get rid of this emptyish feeling.

They returned to the charming little tree-lined city the next day.

When they got there, it was lonely. They arranged their souvenirs on their kitchen window sill.

Mr. Seek stopped asking about Mrs. Seek's tummy, but neither of them stopped thinking about it and how they had been silly to think they could grow a baby in all those hot, cold, and soggy places.

One morning, when they had all but given up hope,
Mrs. Seek noticed that the souvenirs from other
places were thriving in their home—

the orchid from the jungle
was blooming,

the little pine tree from
the mountain was greener
than ever,

and the cactus from the
desert was as prickly as
could be!

How lovely, thought Mrs. Seek, that these growing plants from other places could thrive in her home.

Wait! That idea gave Mrs. Seek
another idea . . .

a new idea . . .

a very good idea!

If an orchid, a cactus, and a pine tree could come from somewhere else, not in her tummy, maybe a baby could too.

What if Mr. and Mrs. Seek had been looking
inside the wrong tummy the whole time?

What if their baby was
growing inside someone
else's tummy?

What if they had been
looking in *here* when they
should have been looking

in there?

The next day Mr. and Mrs. Seek drove just down the road to a place in their charming little city that was more special than any desert or mountain or jungle.

There they met a lovely young lady with a great big tummy. The young lady told them that there was a baby growing in her tummy, and she wanted to place it with two very special parents.

Can you guess who those very special parents were?
That's right—Mr. and Mrs. Seek!

Mr. and Mrs. Seek's baby had been growing
in a tummy all along—just someone else's!

It all made sense. And it wasn't long after that their baby was born and came home to live with them, calling them "Mommy" and "Daddy" ever since, and filling that old *emptyish* feeling with something that looked *weirdly* like happiness.

TRACEY ZEECK was born in Texas and raised in Oklahoma City, where she currently owns a boutique public relations firm specializing in clients with good business practices and better stories to tell. She has lived in Boulder, CO, Phoenix, AZ, and briefly in Pittsburgh, PA, always working in her chosen vocation of public relations, which allows her to share her creativity through storytelling, and to keep those writing chops honed. She and her husband were lucky enough to become parents through adoption in November 2007 and have been on a mission to tell the world their family's love story ever since. *The Not In Here Story* is the ever-evolving origin tale of her little family.

DAVID BIZZARO is a Puppeteer, Illustrator, and Funny Video Maker living in NYC. He believes you can do anything you set your mind to as long as you have a positive outlook. When David is not making puppets or silly videos, he is spending time with his wife Cassie and his cat Rita. Or he is making more puppets. He might have too many.